BRIGHT and EARLY BOOKS
for BEGINNING Beginners

# This book belongs to ...

_____

# Love STINKS!

*For my loves—Danny, Kate, and Jane*
*—D.M.*

*For my mom, Anita,*
*whose constant warmth and support*
*I could not repay, but I'll try anyway*
*—G.W.*


This edition published by Sandvik Publishing.
Originally published as a Step into Reading book in the United States by Random House Children's Books, a division of Penguin Random House LLC, in 2022.



Printed in Melrose Park, Illinois, U.S.A.

Item #: 00001921

SP20002116OCT2023

Early Moments Edition

First Printing, October 2023

# Love STINKS!

by Diana Murray

illustrated by Gal Weizman

**A Bright and Early Book**
From BEGINNER BOOKS®
A Division of Random House

Dog love.

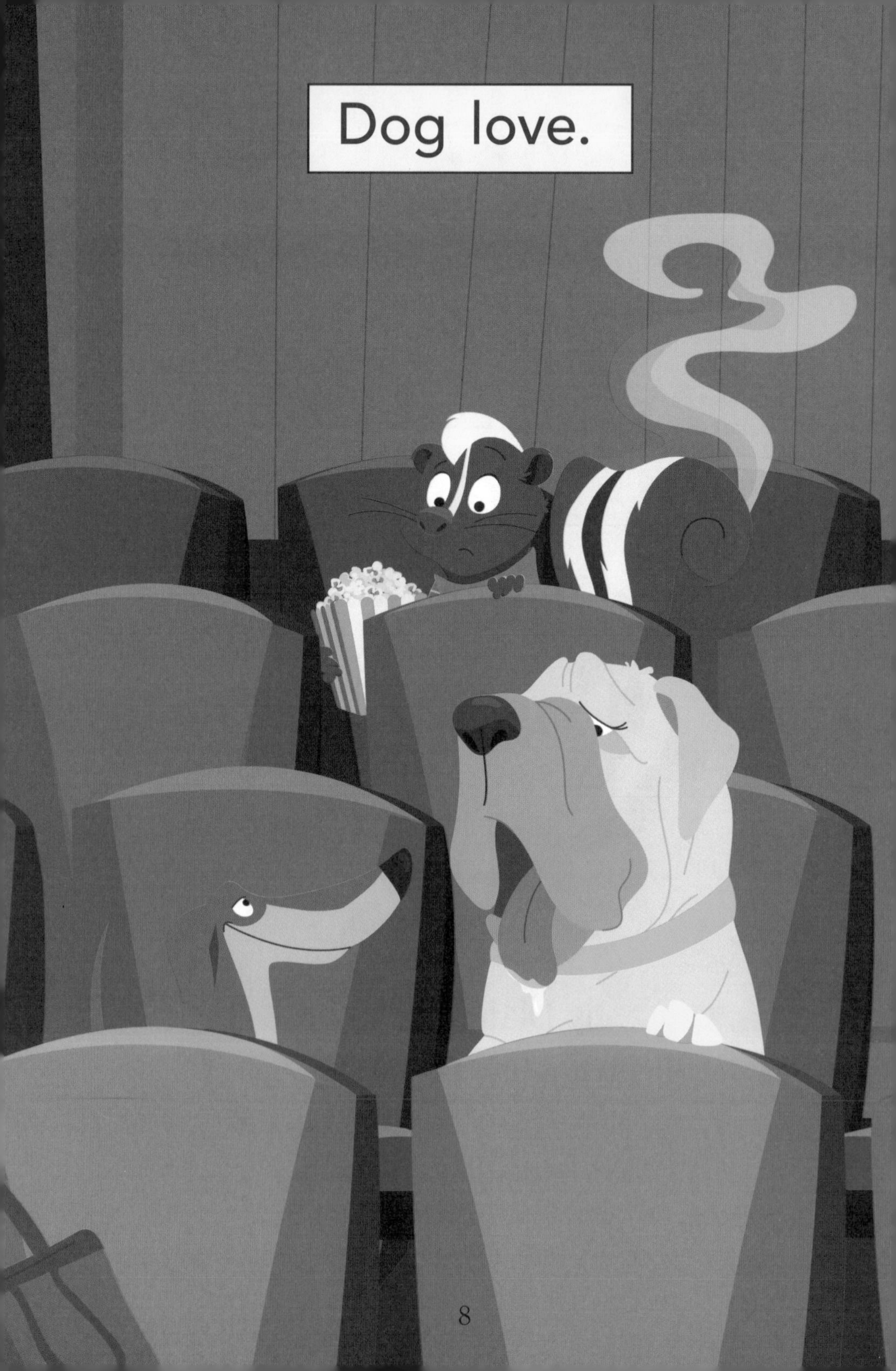

Cat love.

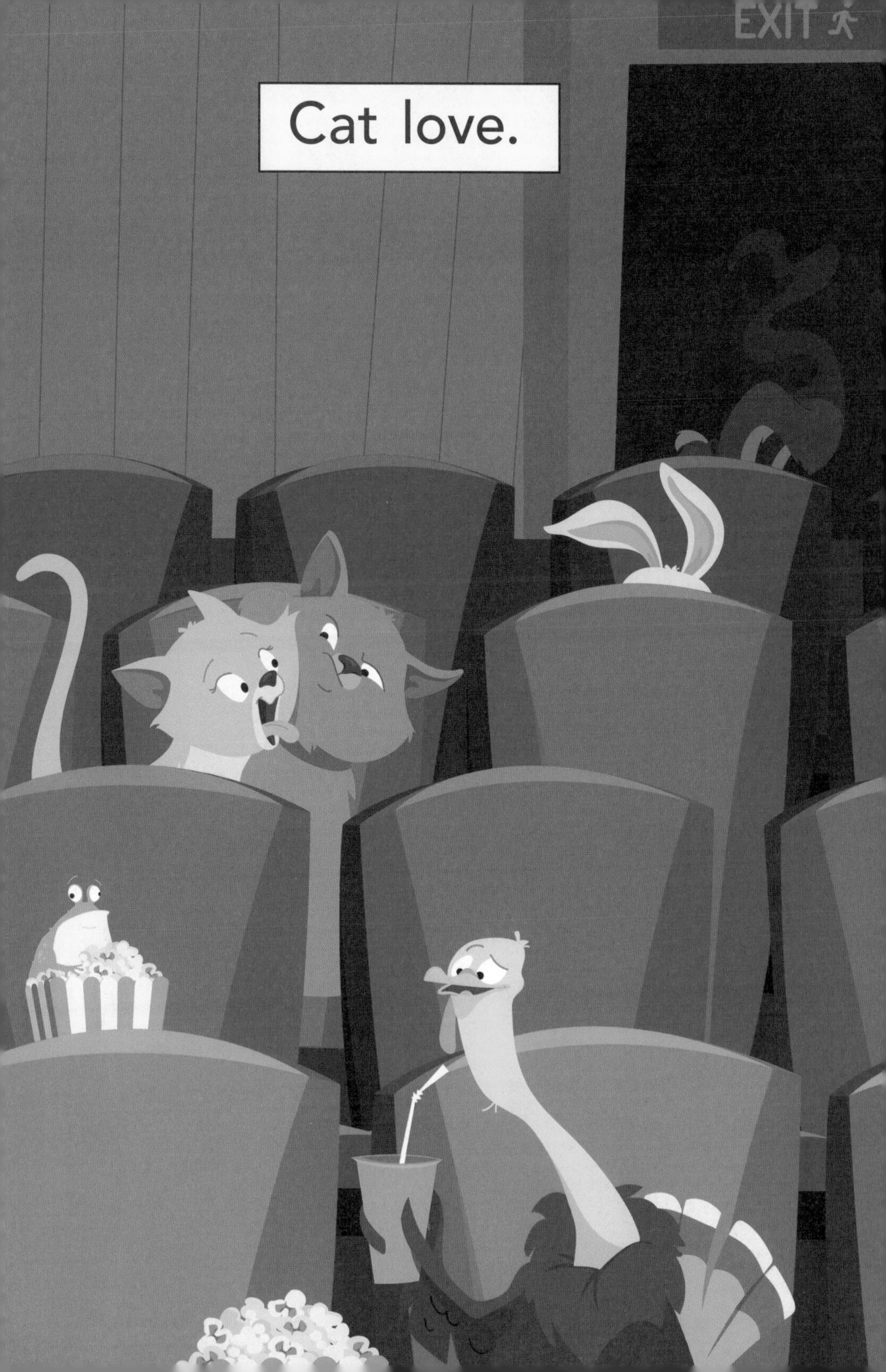
EXIT

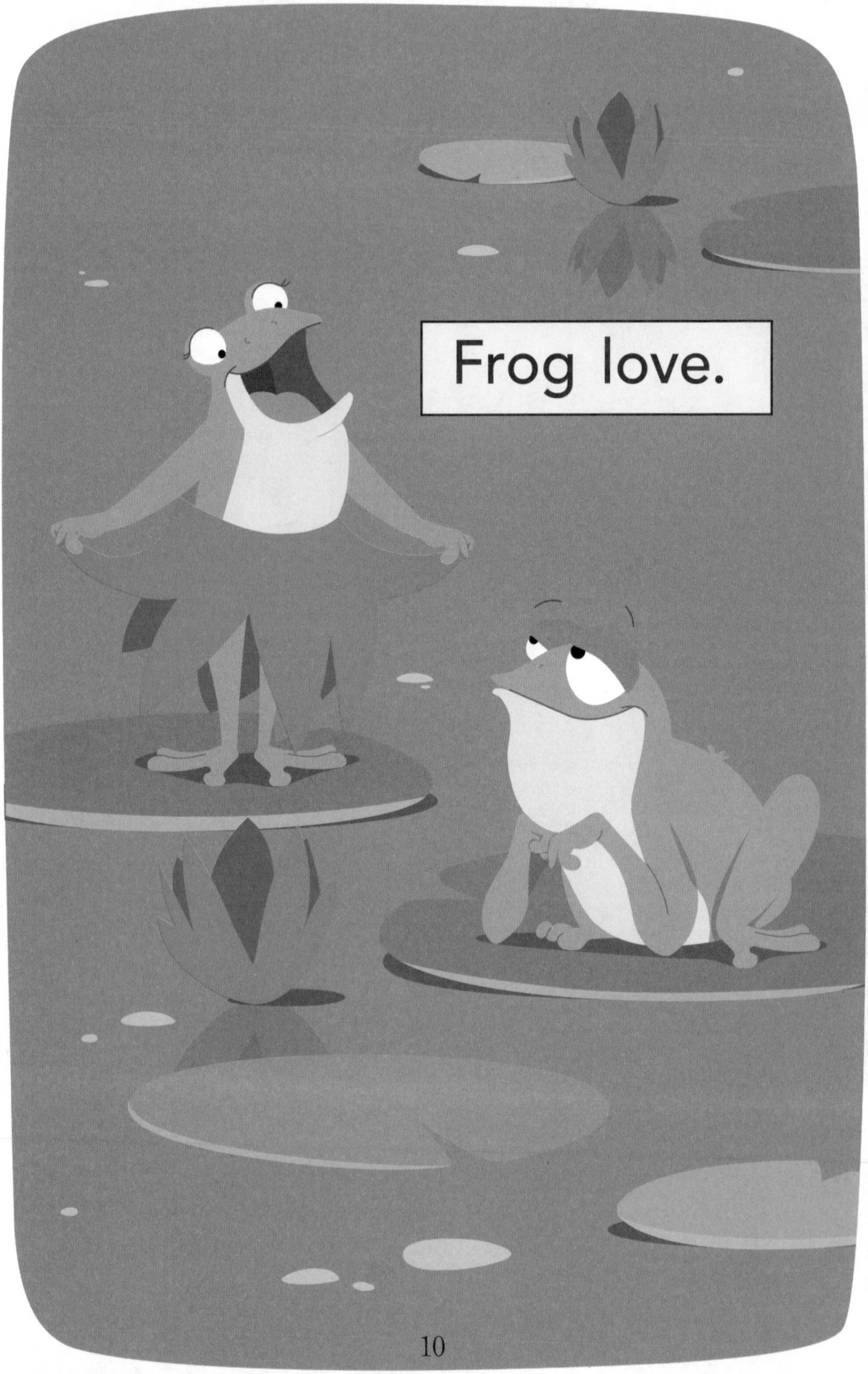
Frog love.

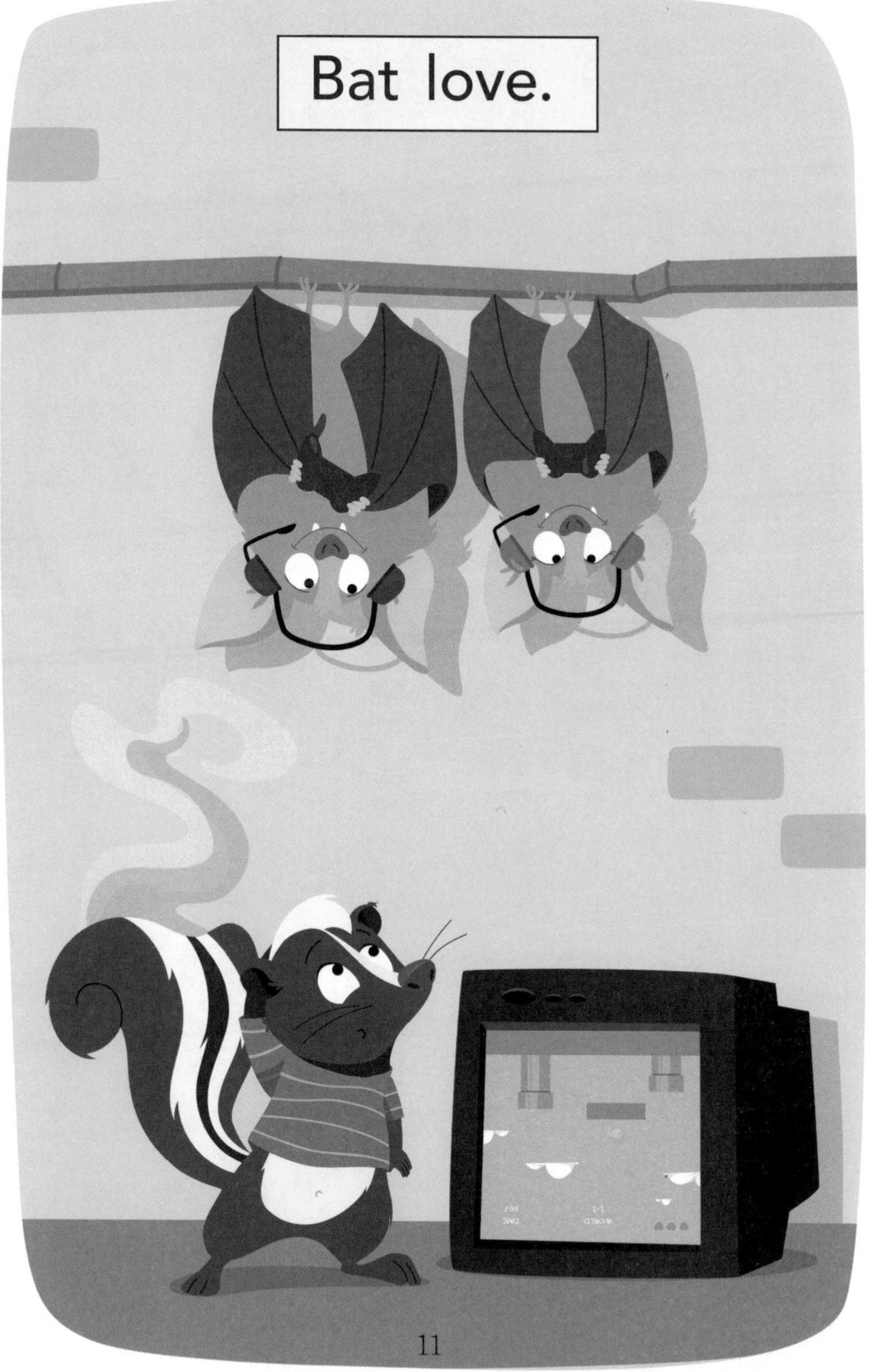
Bat love.

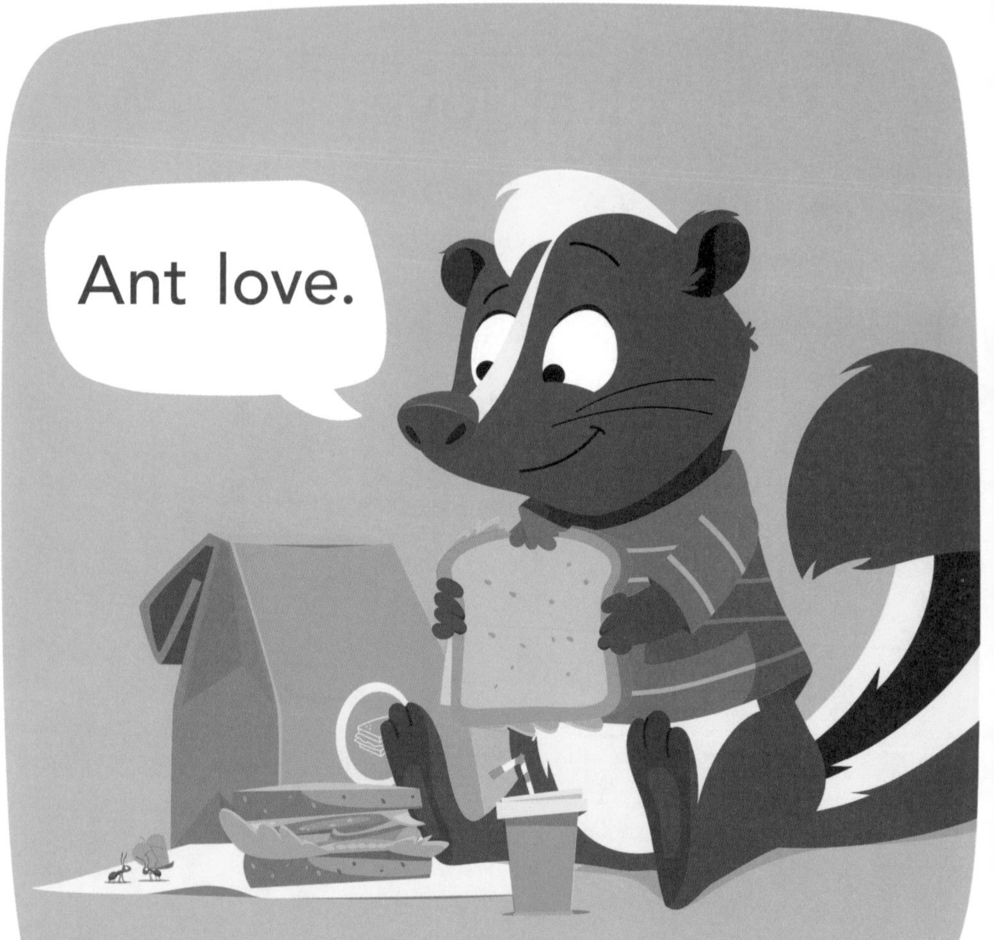
Ant love.

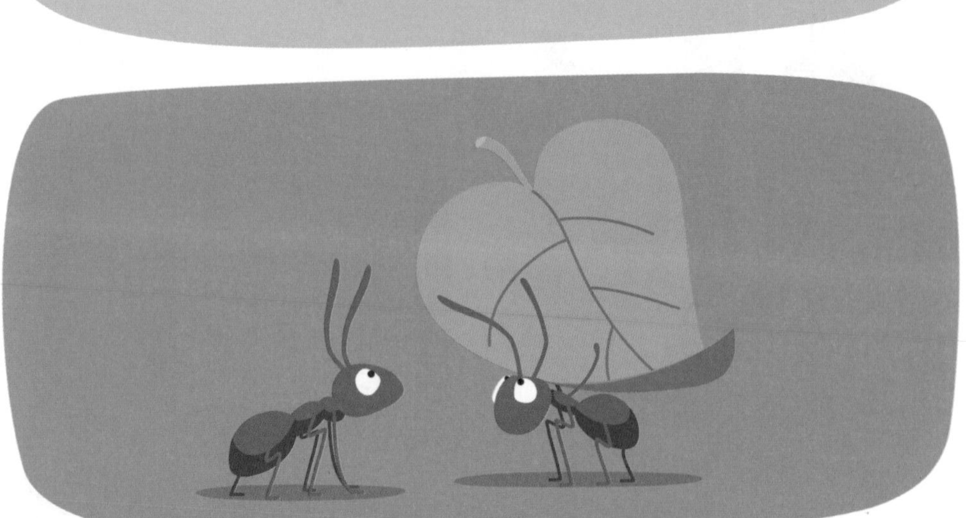

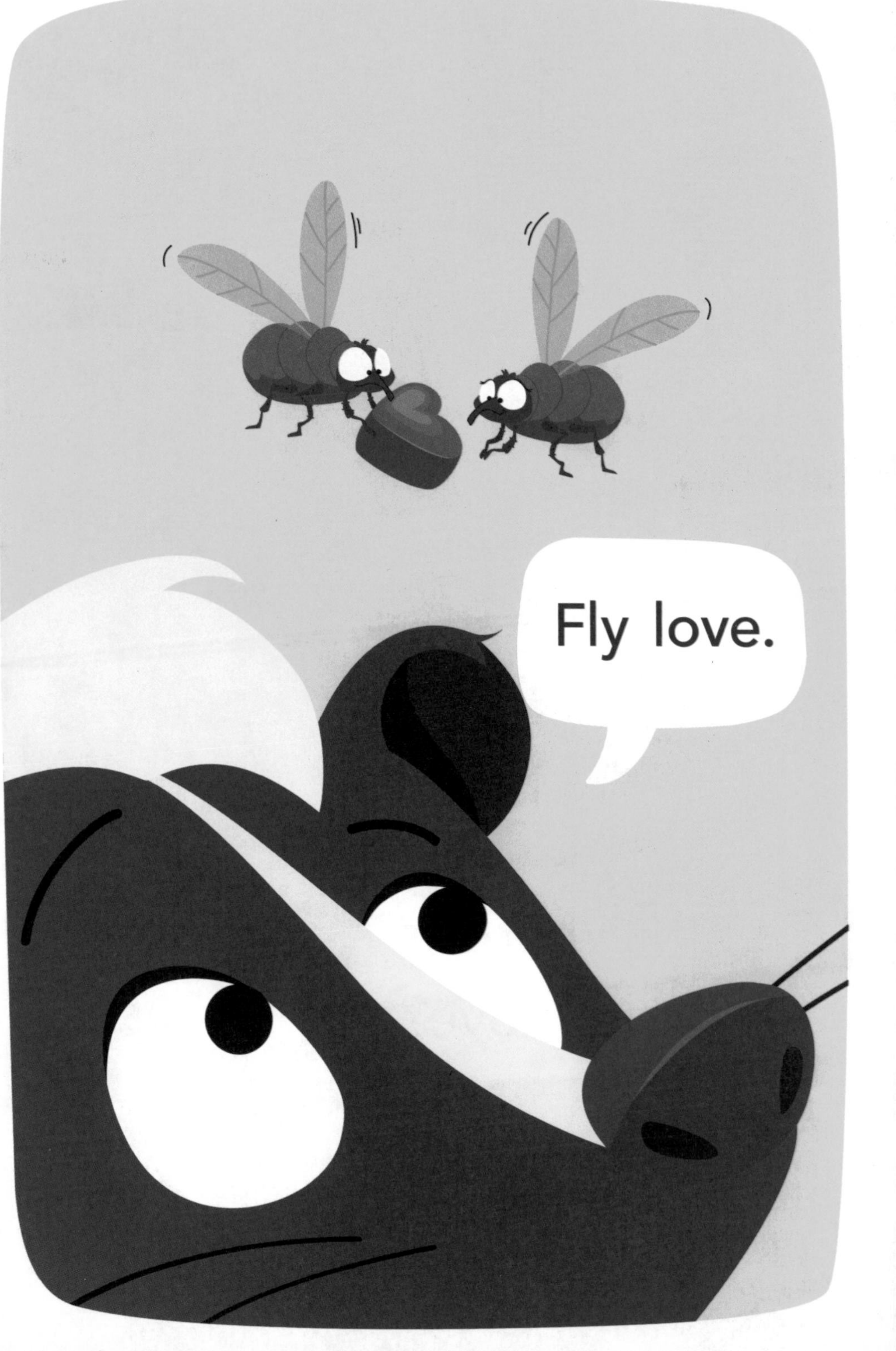
Fly love.

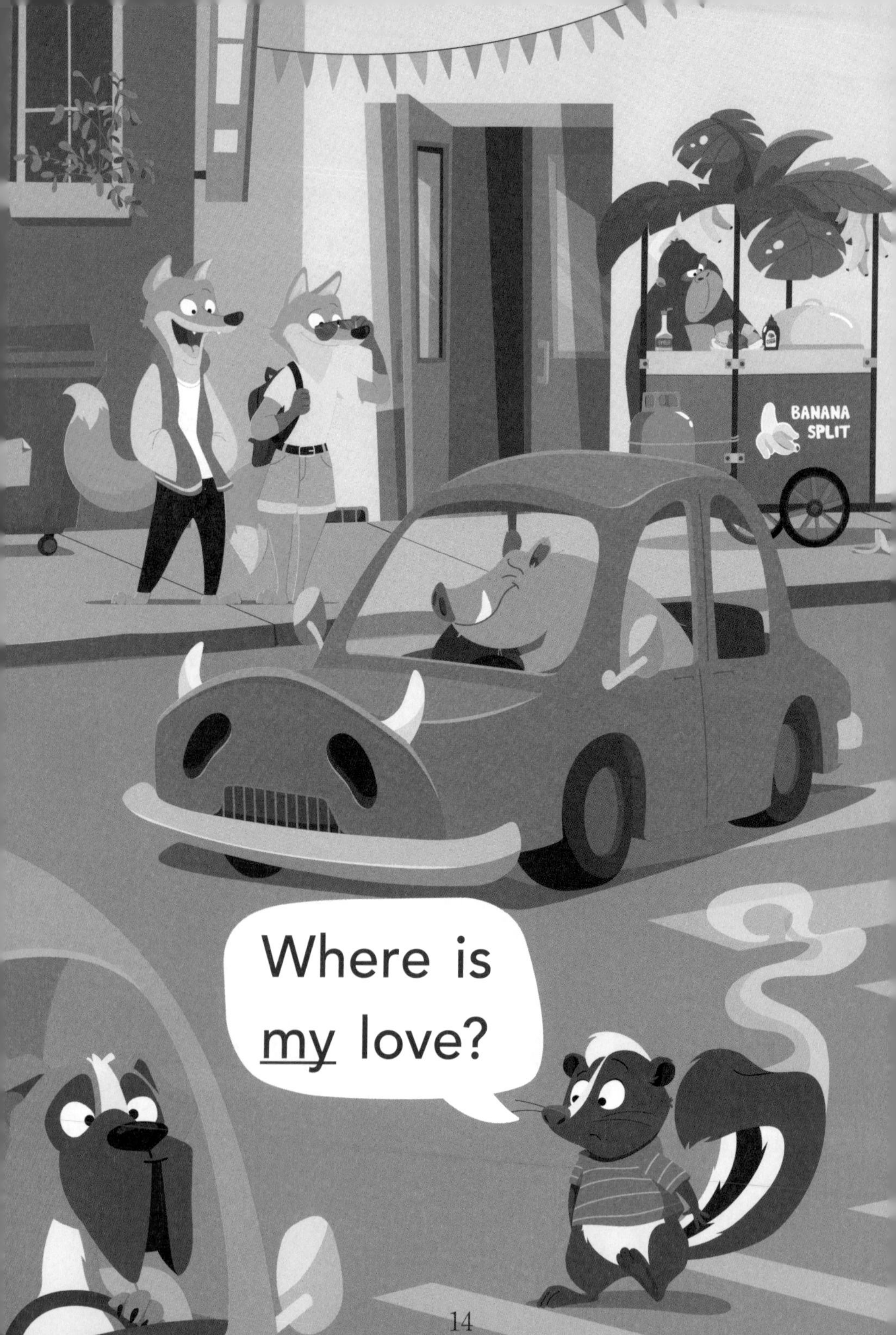
BANANA SPLIT
Where is my love?

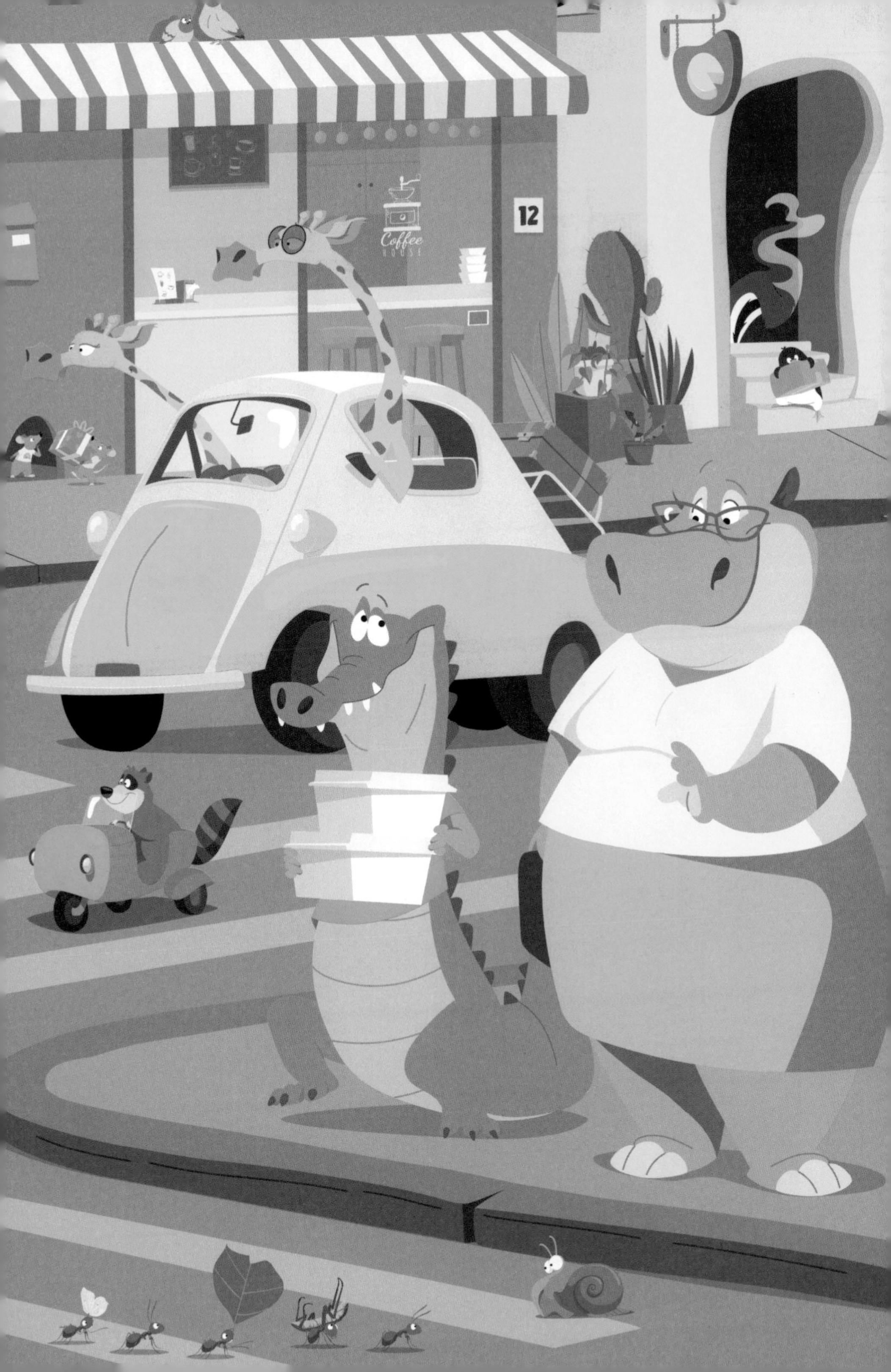
12
Coffee
HOUSE

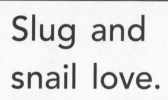

Slug and
snail love.

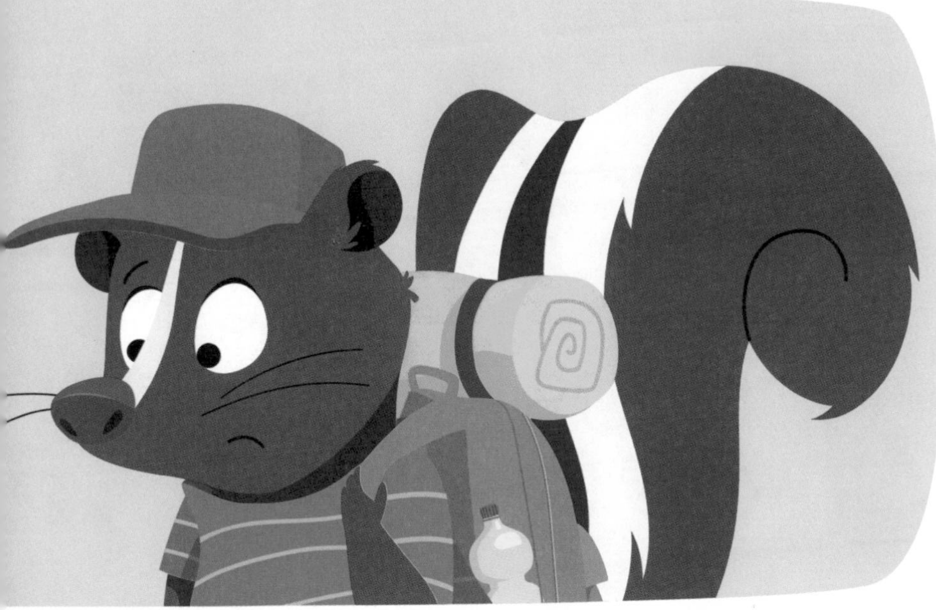
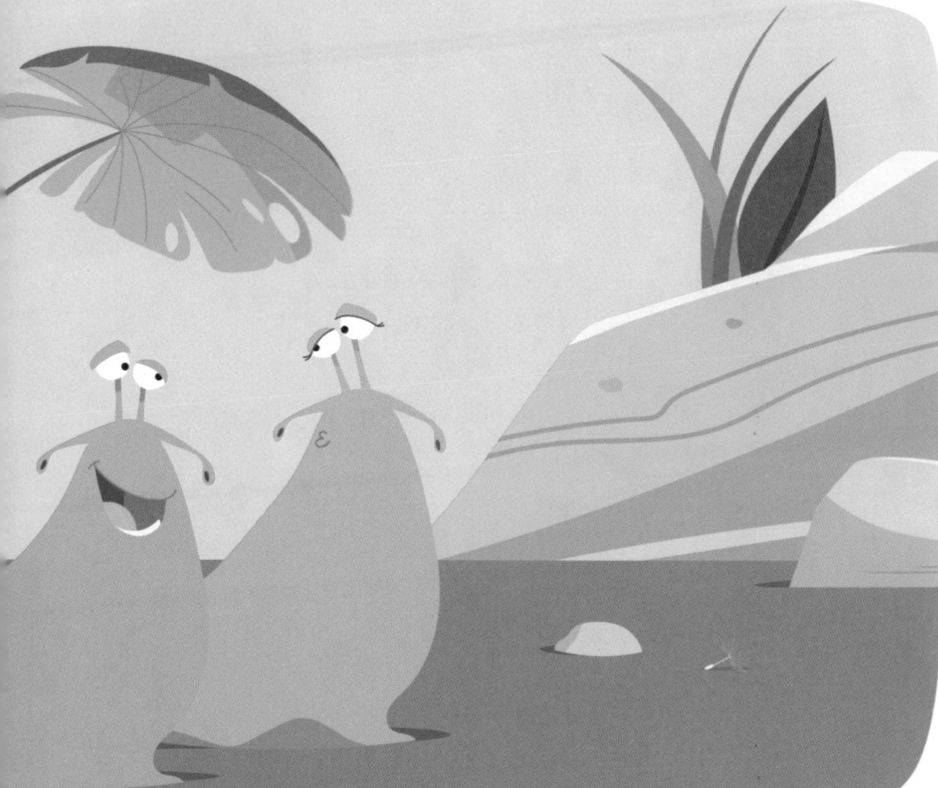

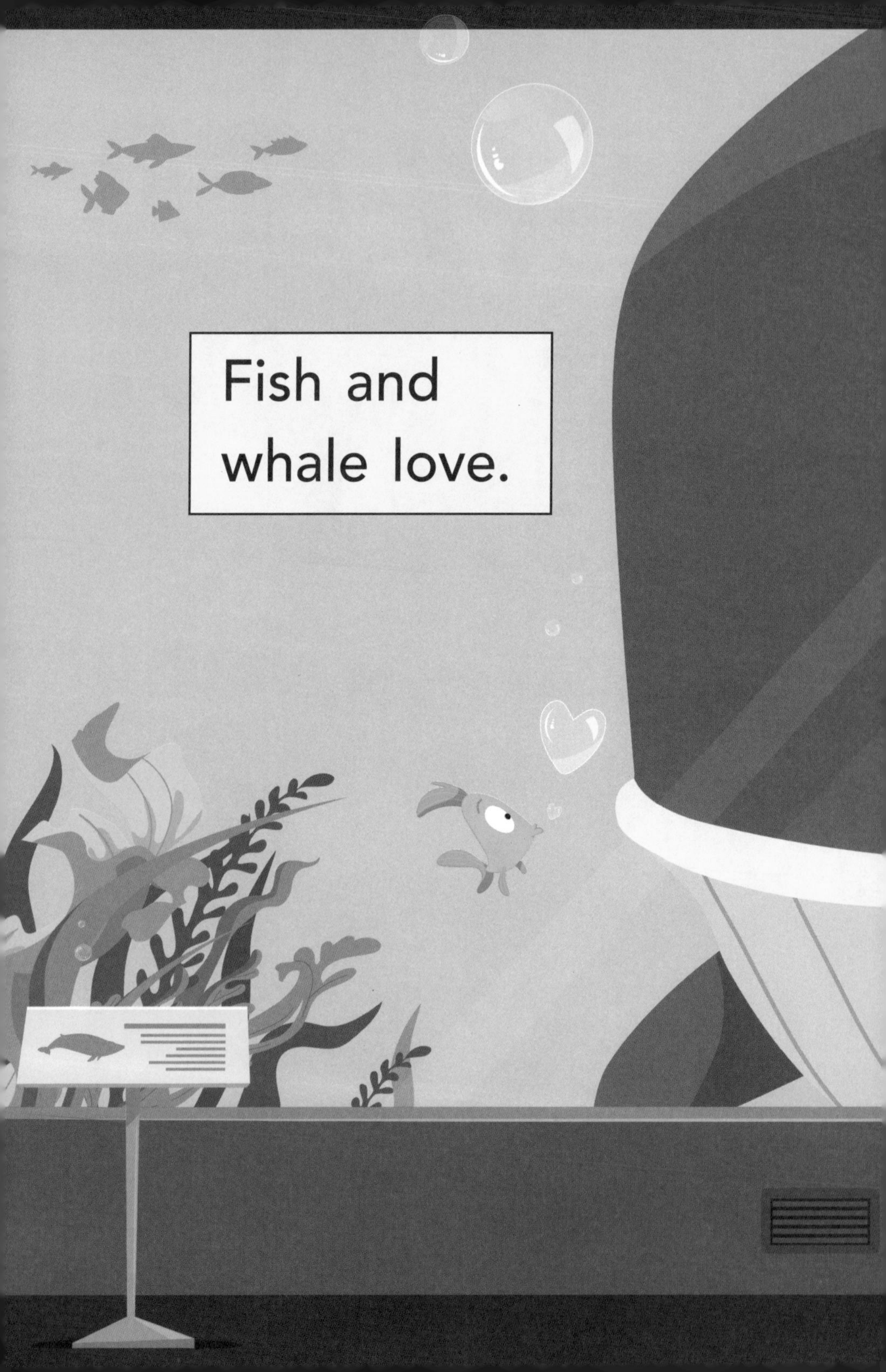

Fish and whale love.

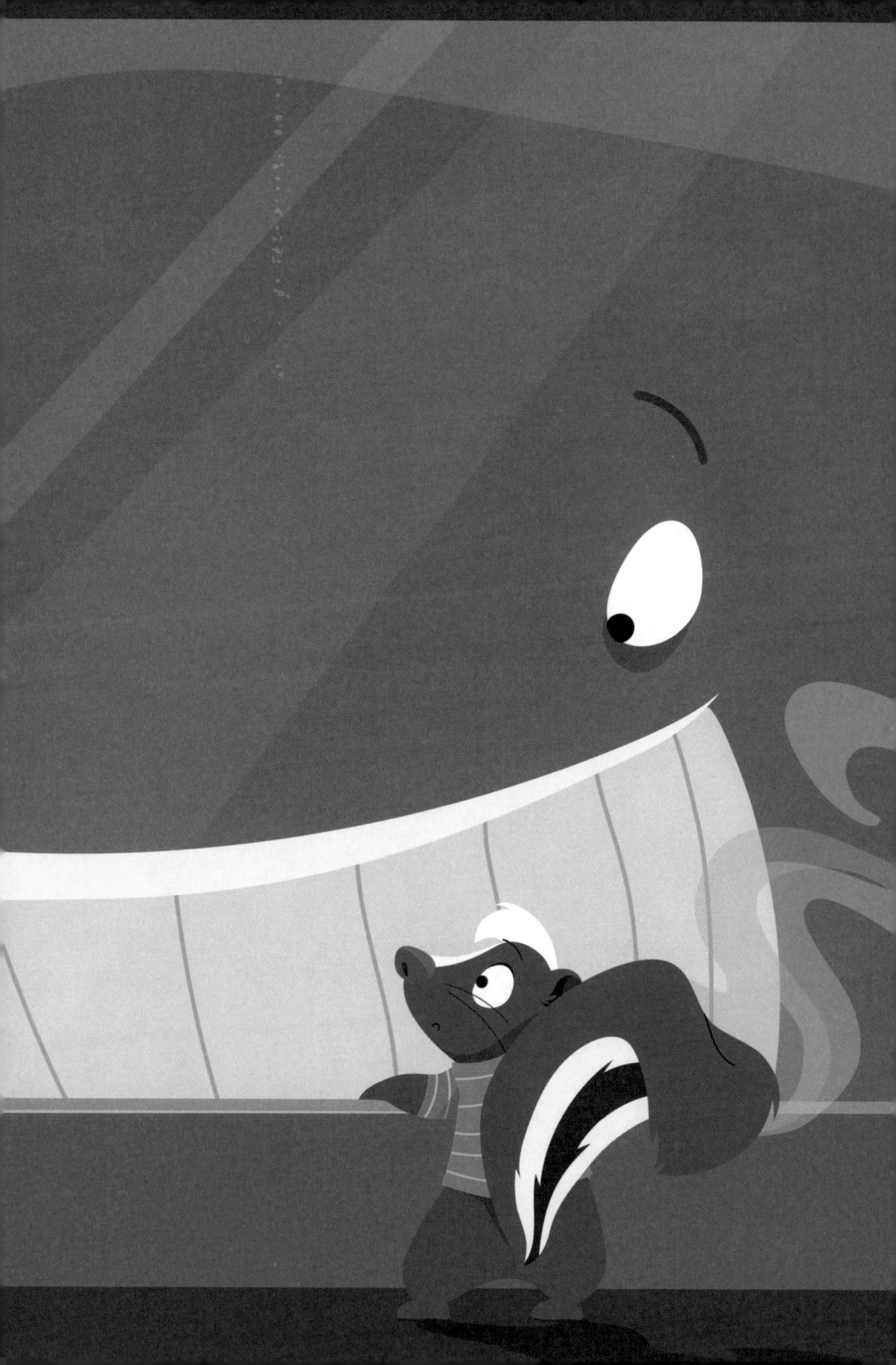

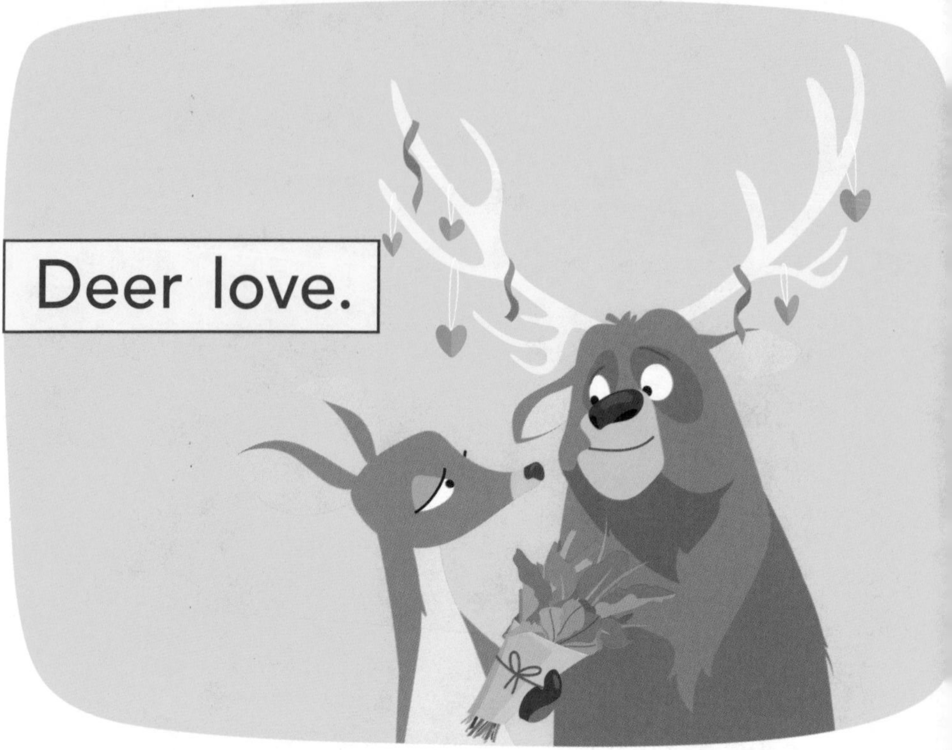
Deer love.

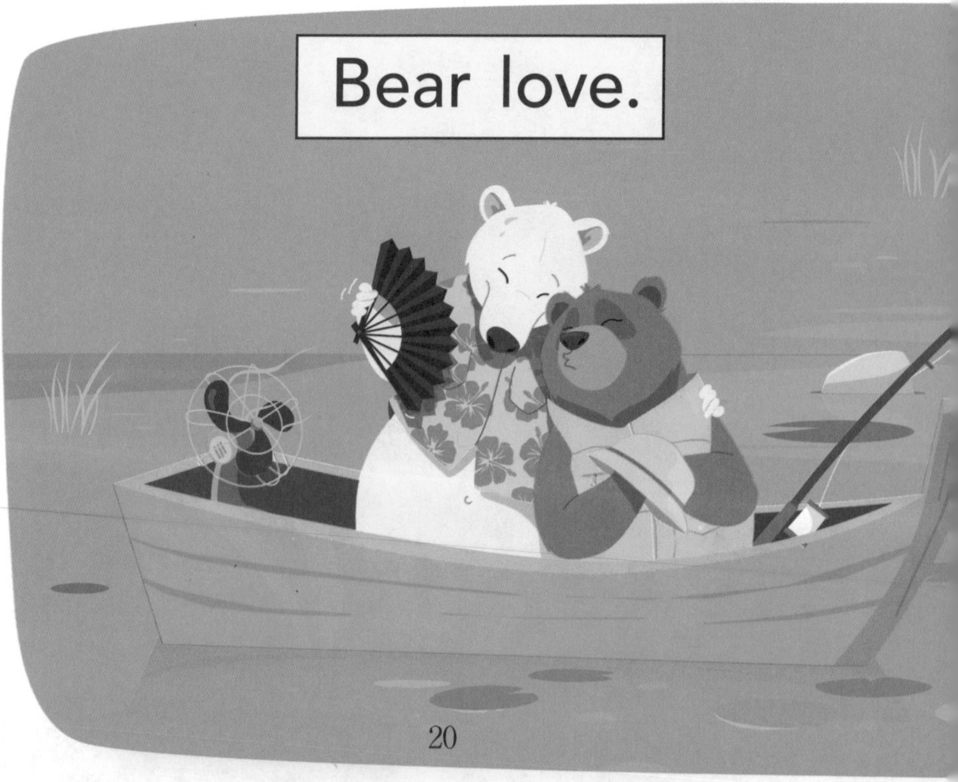
Bear love.

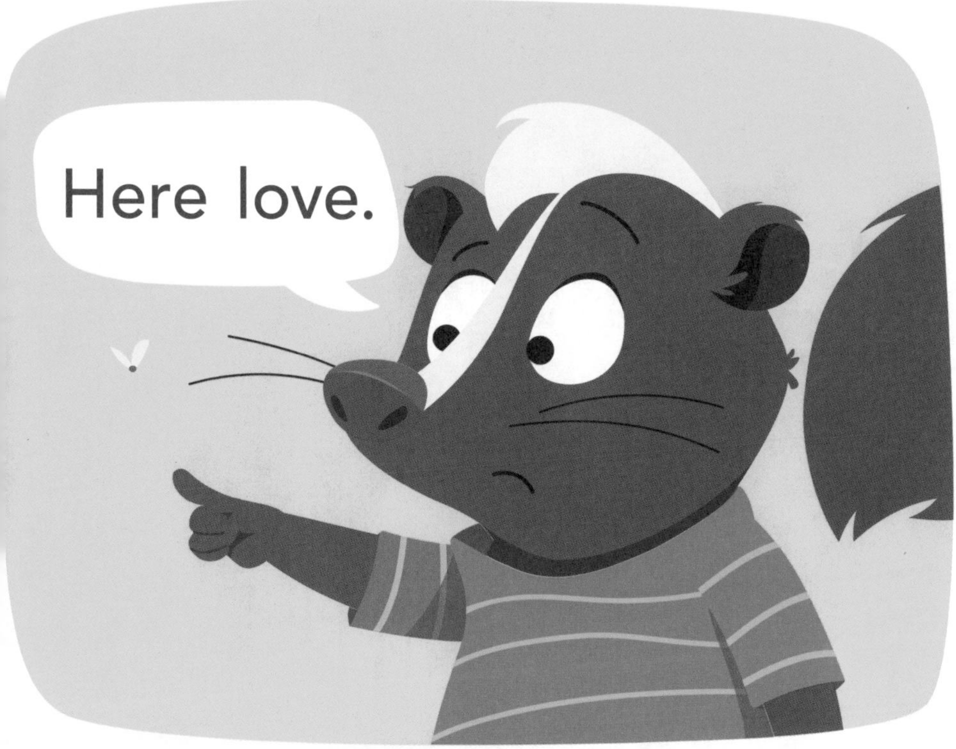
Here love.

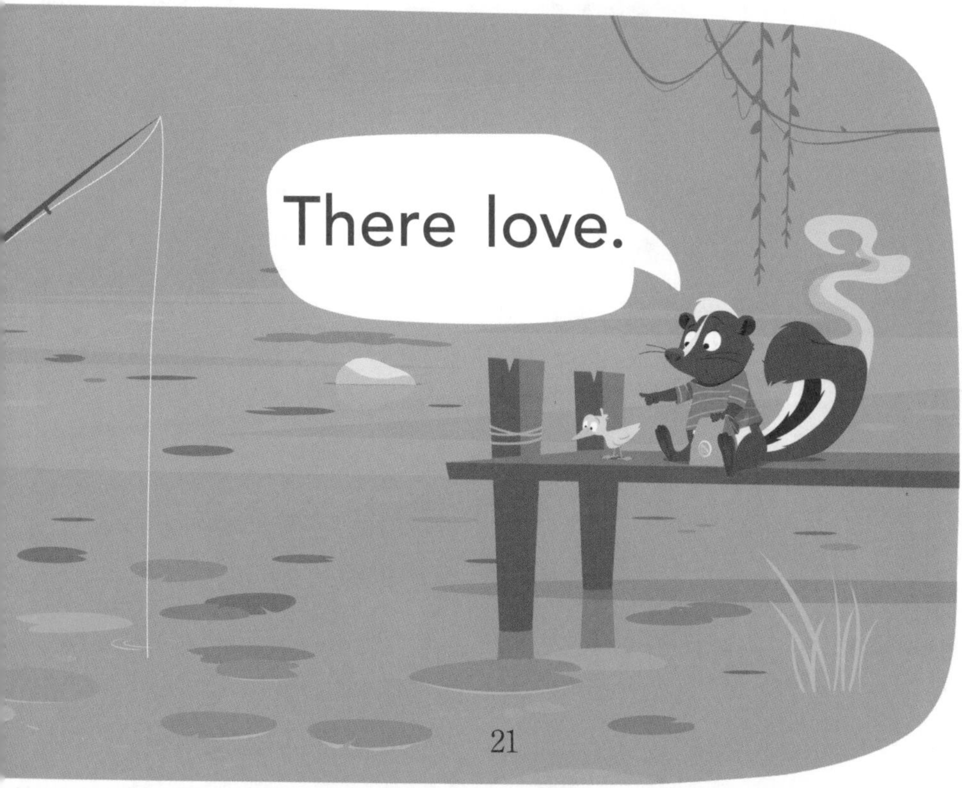
There love.

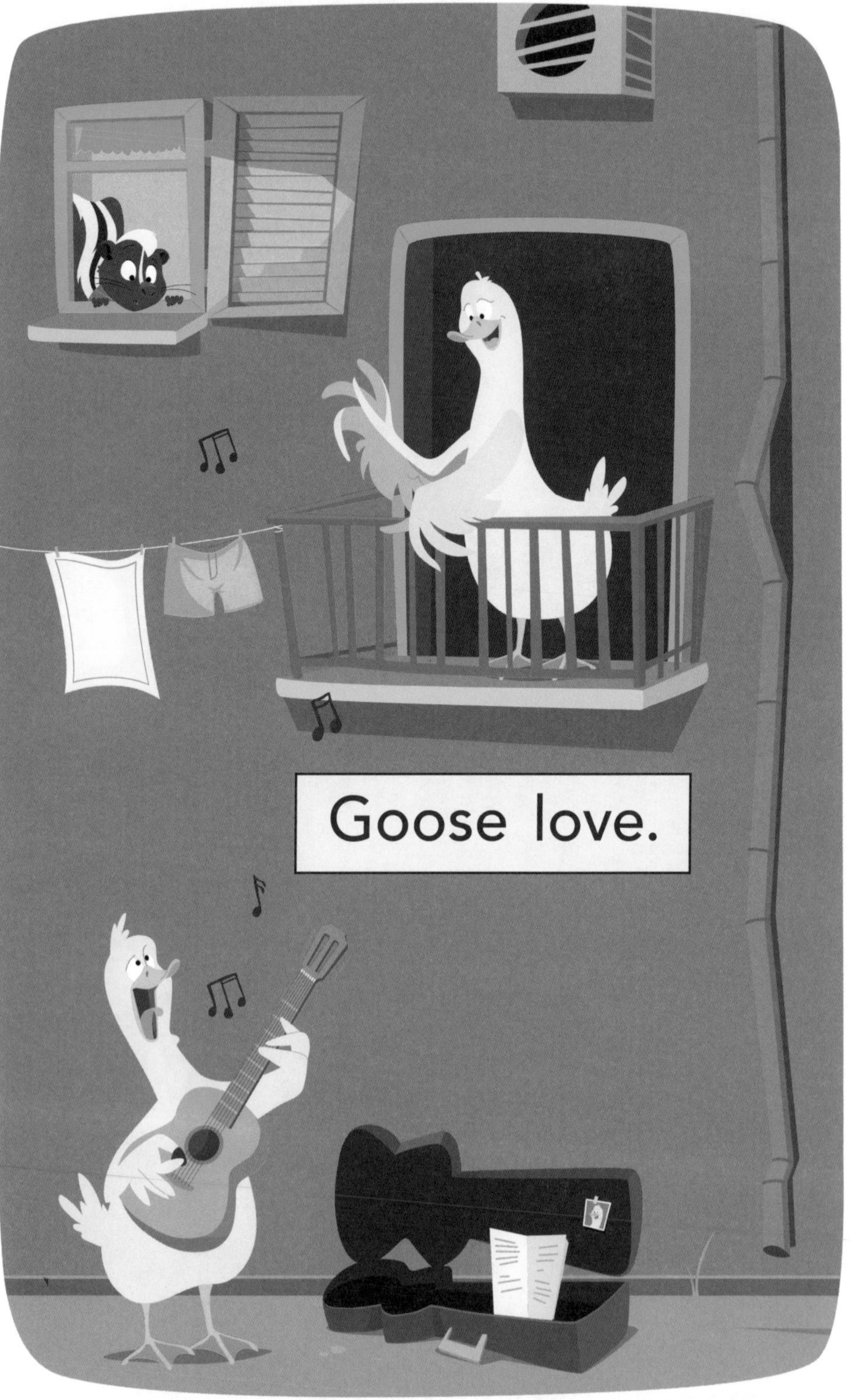

Goose love.

Rat love.

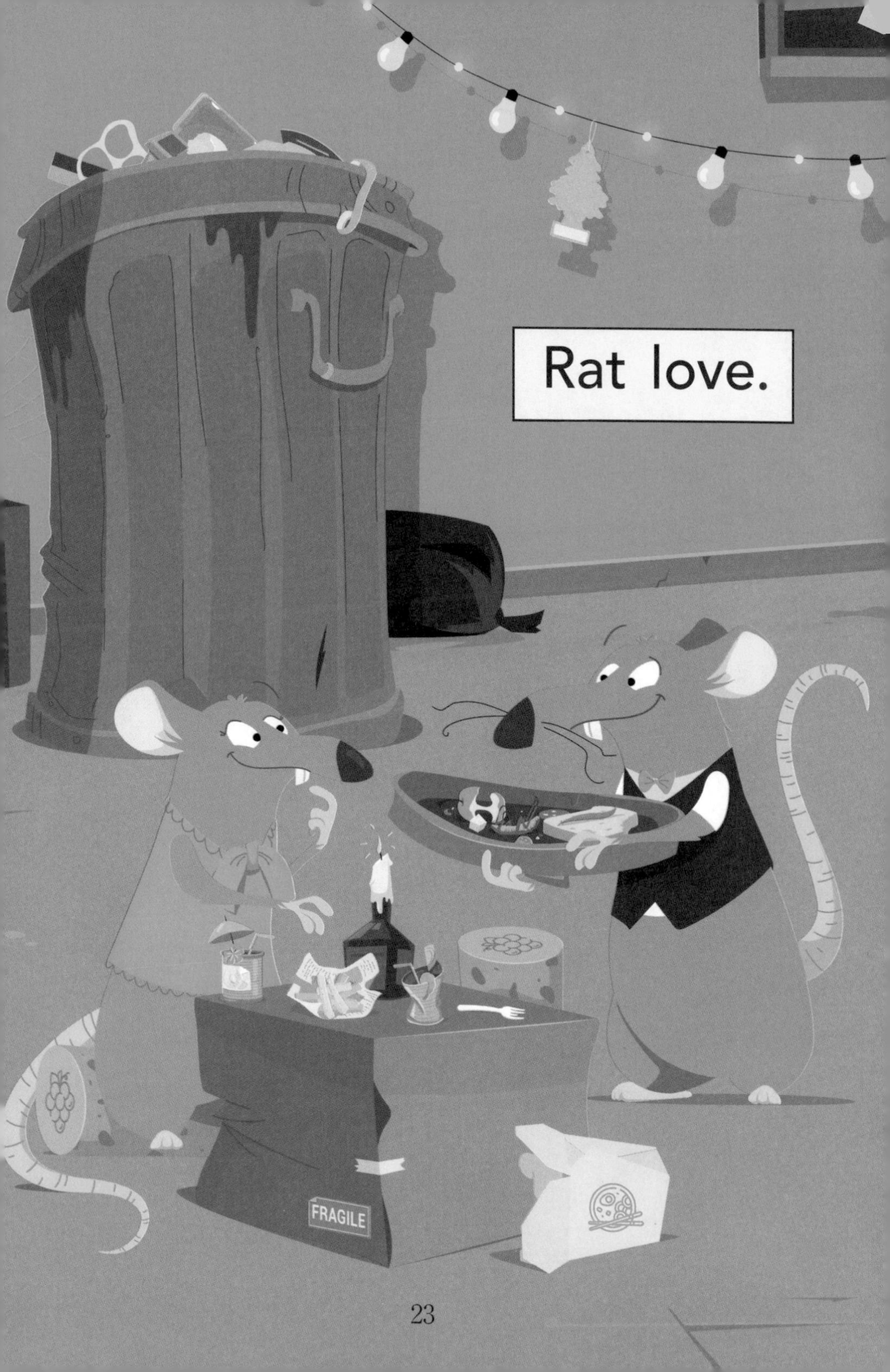
FRAGILE

Moose love.

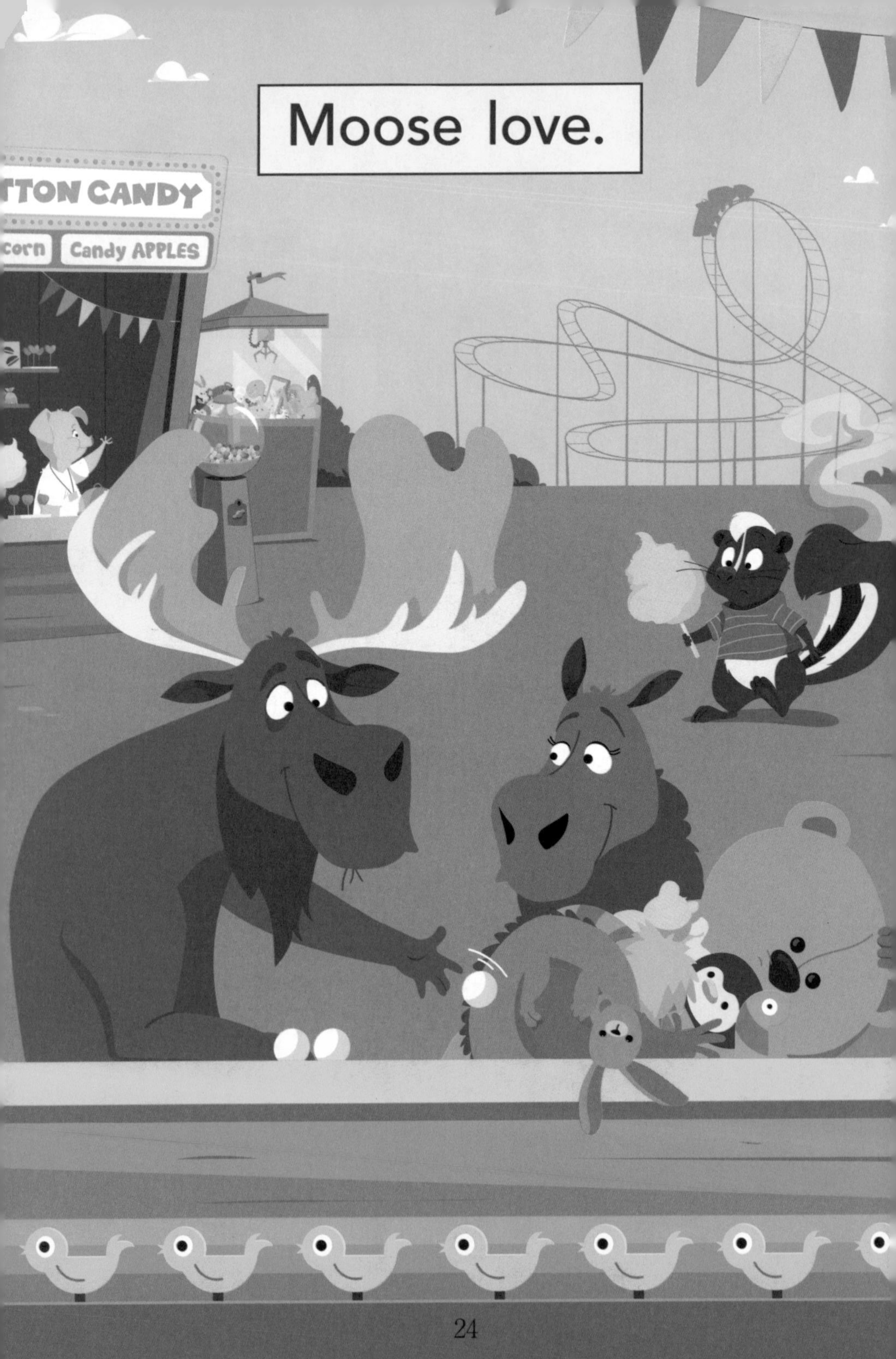
Candy APPLES

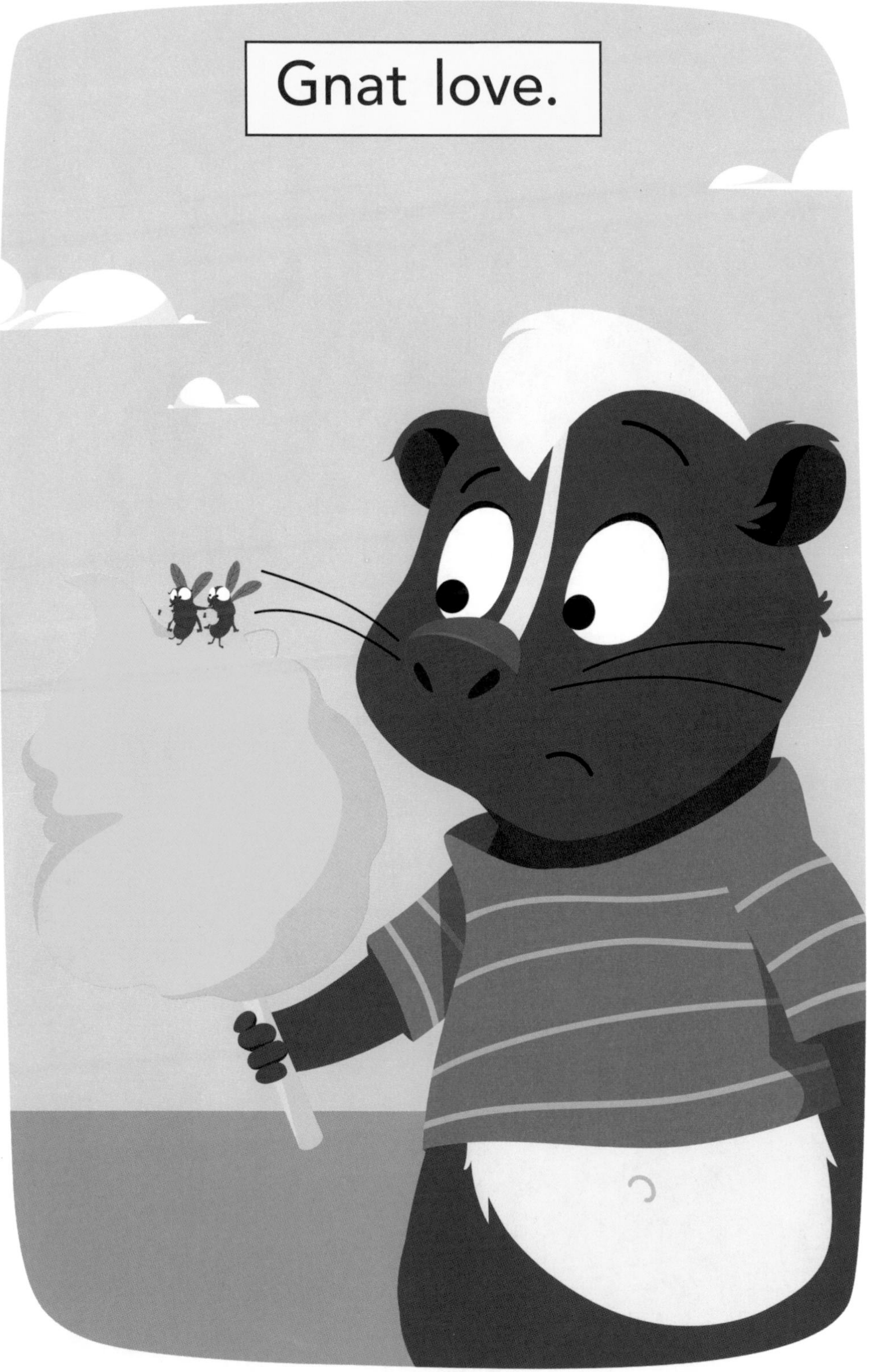
Gnat love.

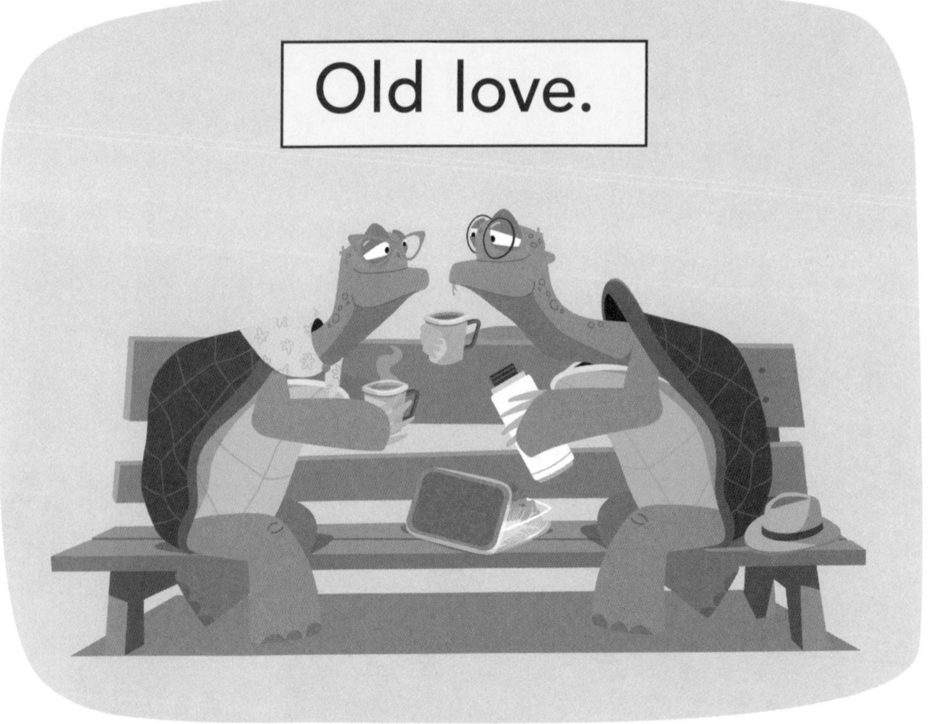
Old love.

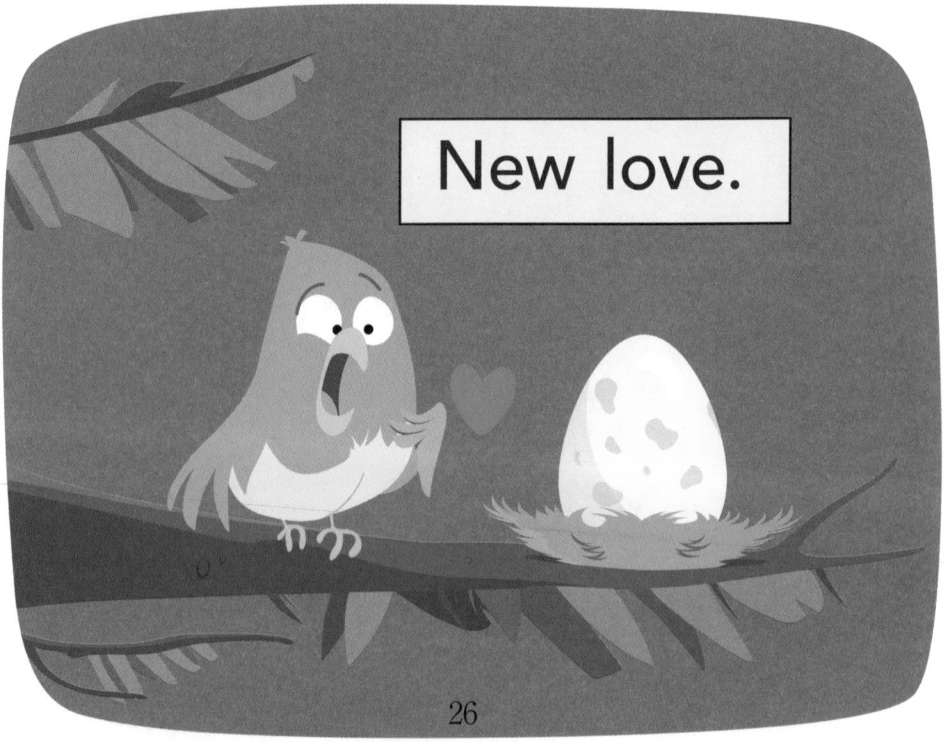
New love.

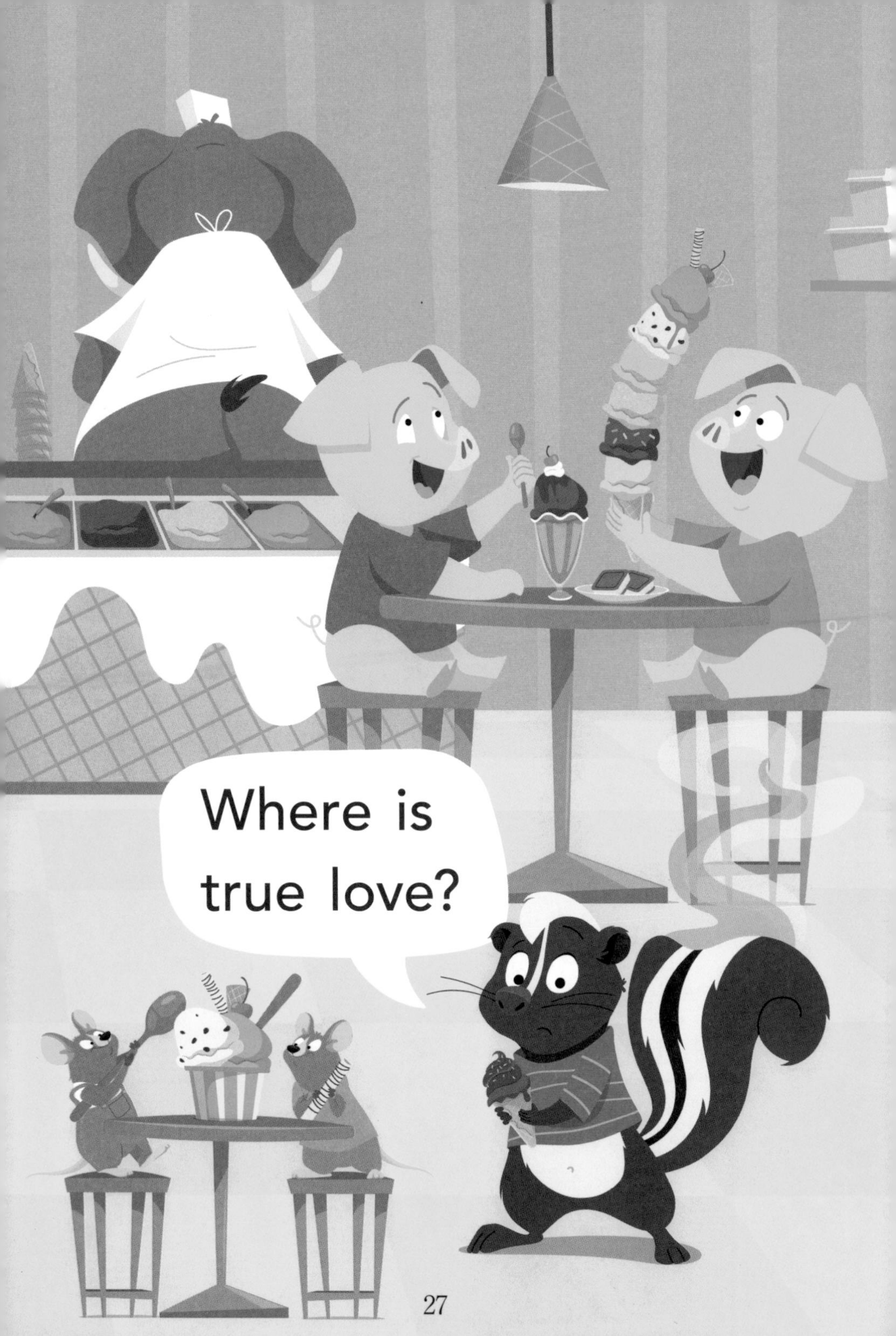
Where is true love?

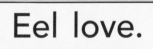

Eel love.

Bee love.

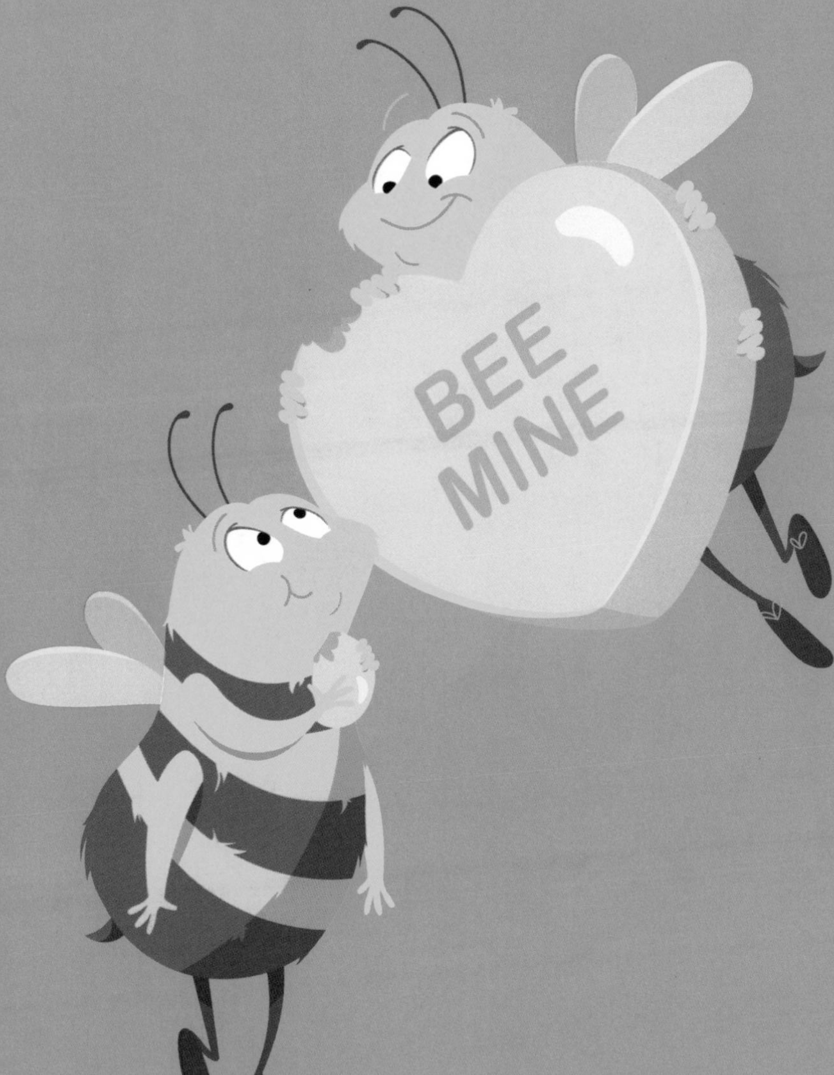
BEE
MINE

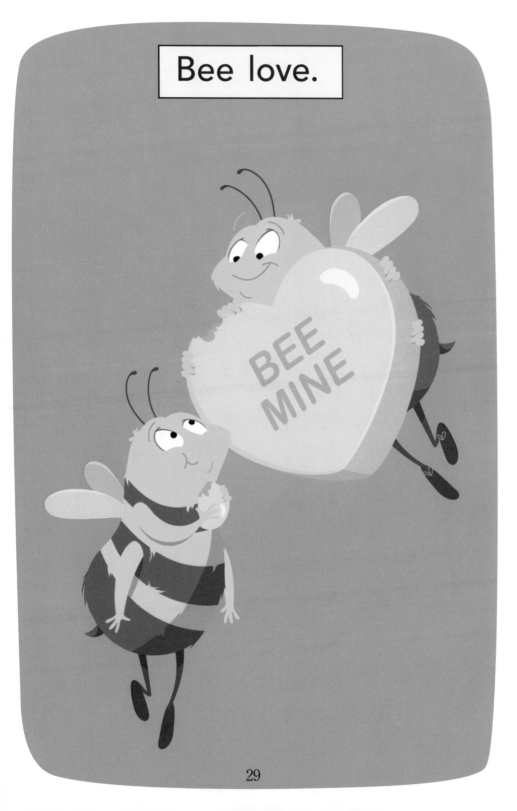

Seal love.

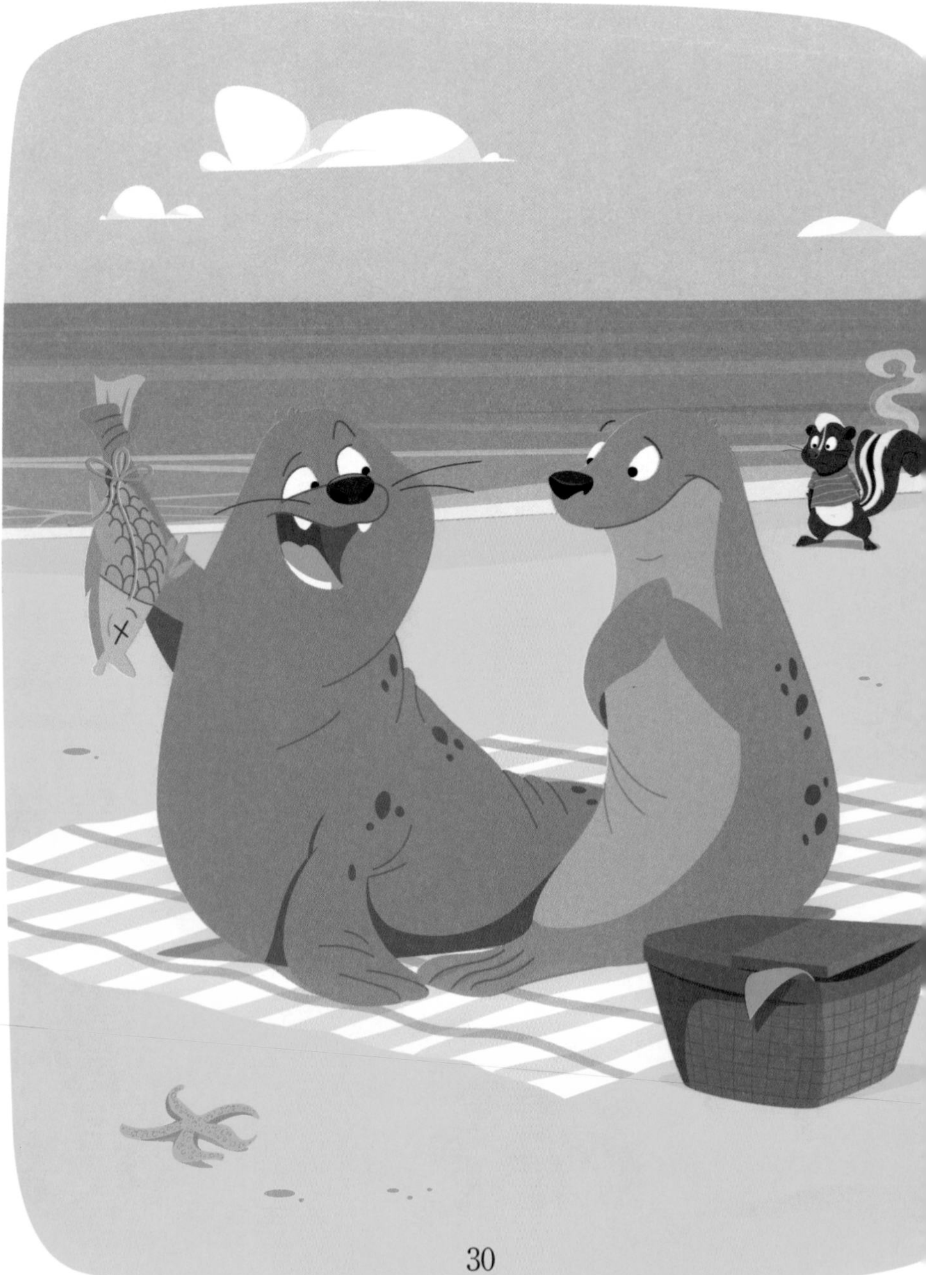

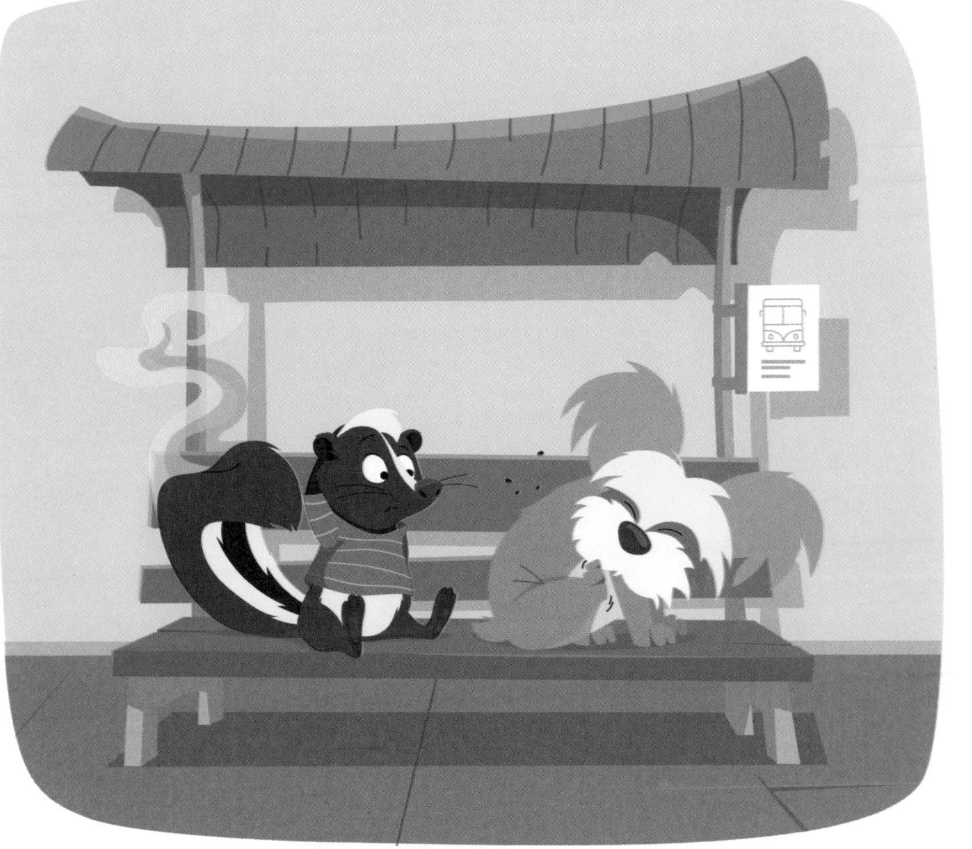

Flea love.

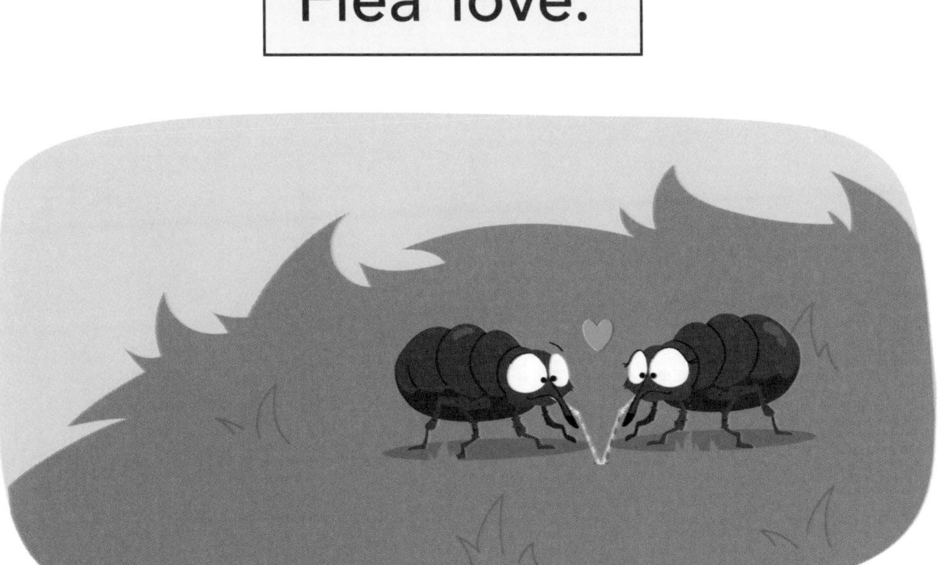

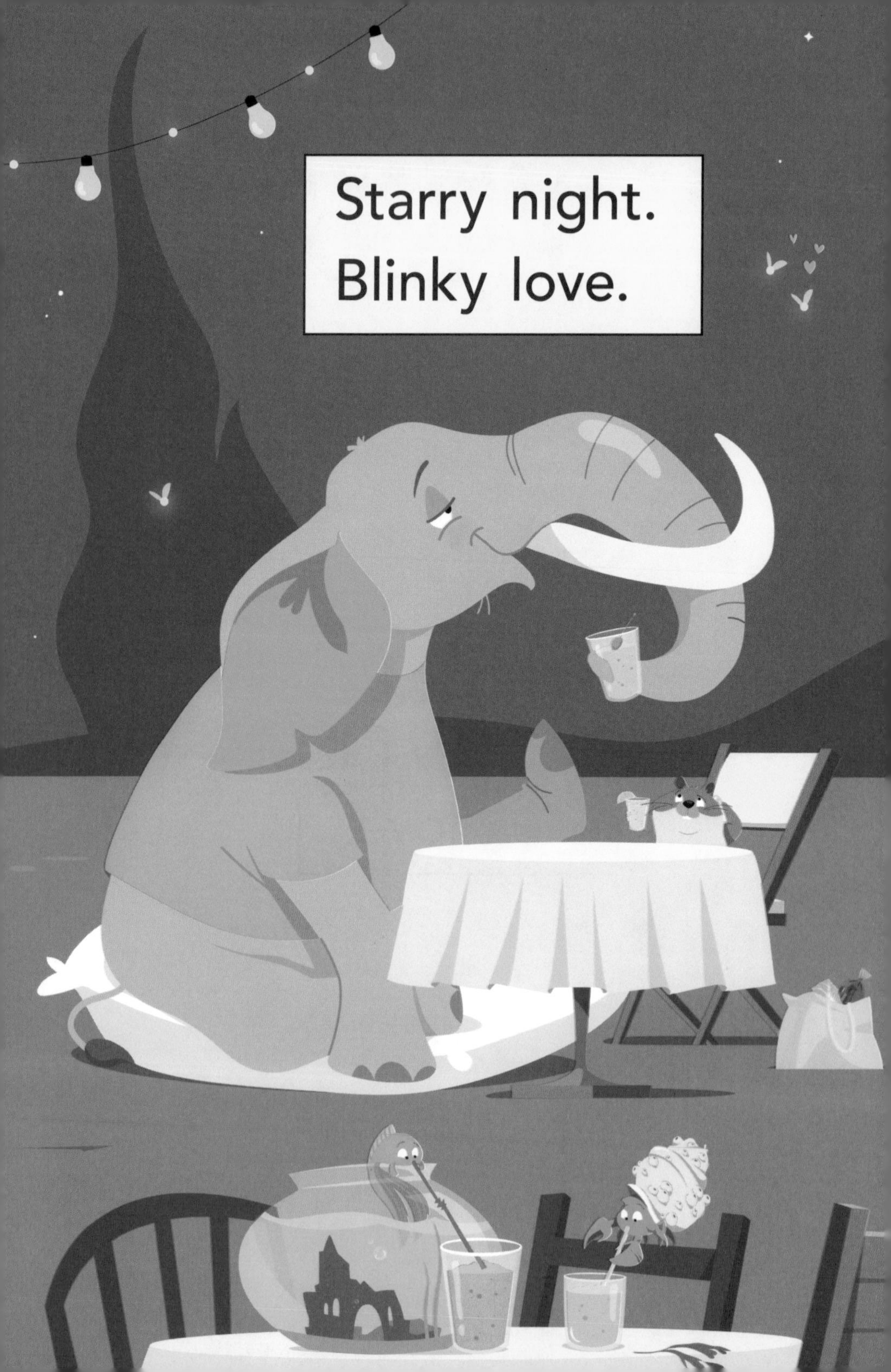
Starry night.
Blinky love.

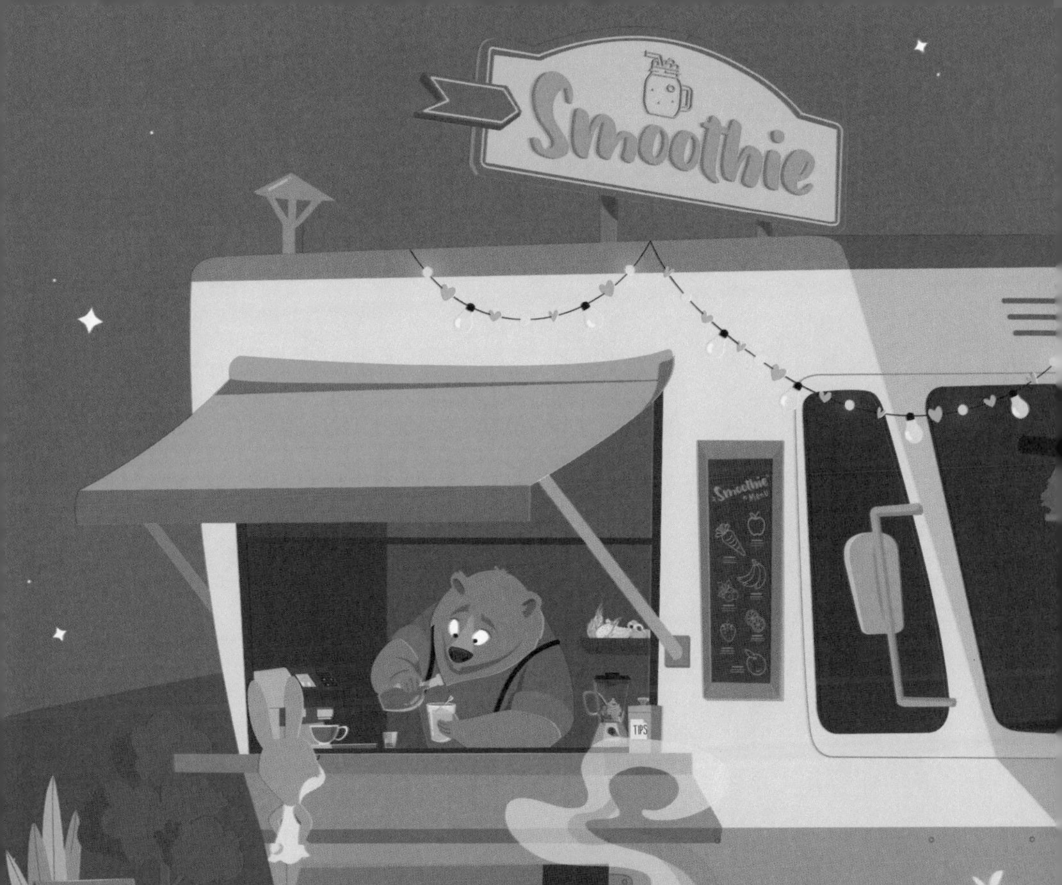
Smoothie
Smoothie Menu
TIPS
Smoothie Menu

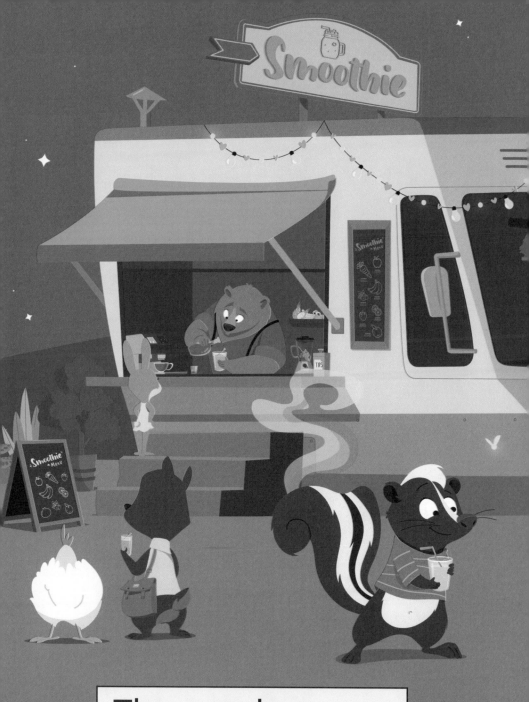

Then, at last . . .

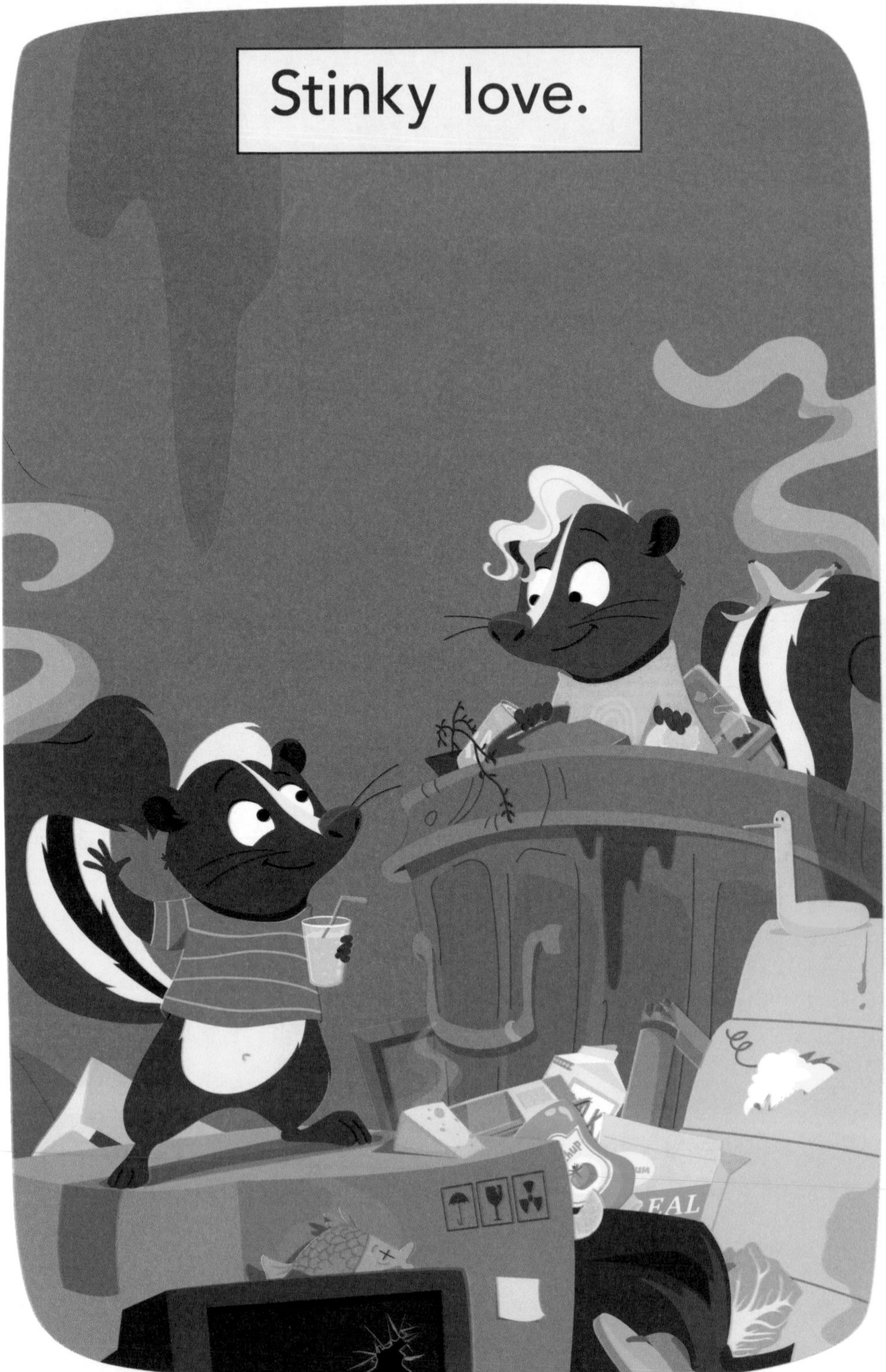
Stinky love.

Hearts glow.
Eyes shine.

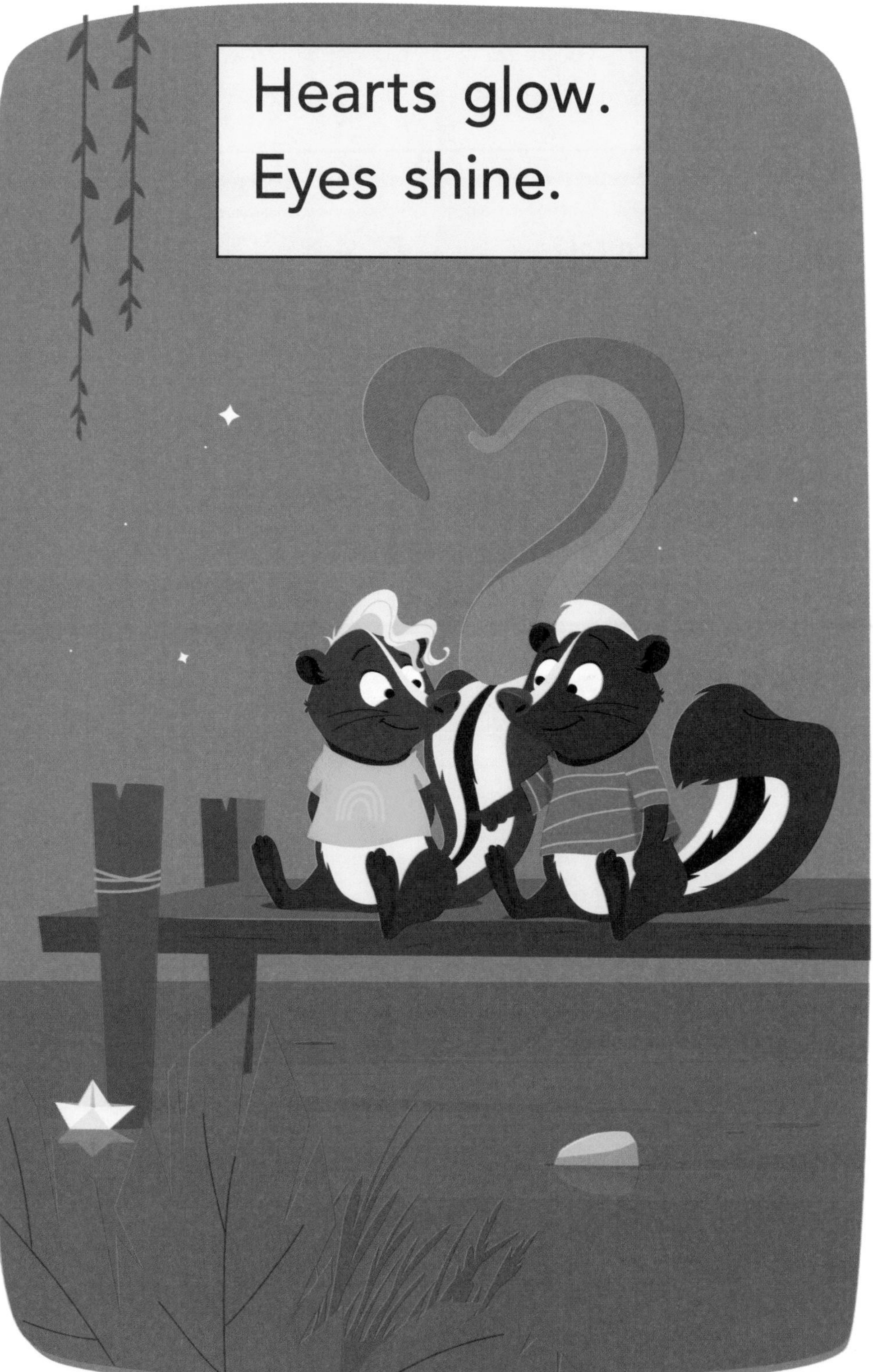

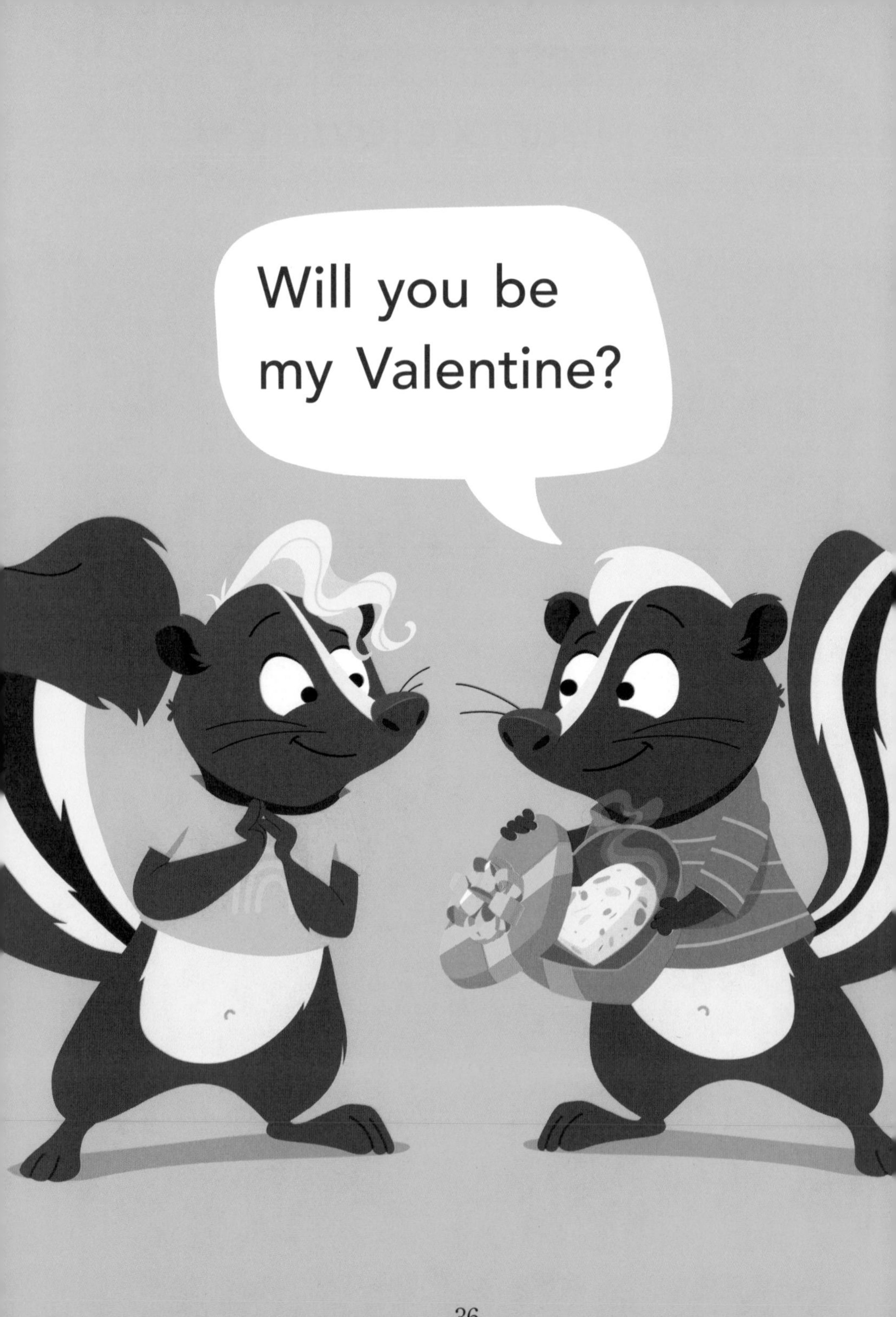
Will you be my Valentine?

BRIGHT and EARLY BOOKS
for BEGINNING Beginners

BRIGHT and EARLY BOOKS
for BEGINNING Beginners
BRIGHT and EARLY BOOKS
for BEGINNING Beginners
BRIGHT and EARLY BOOKS
for BEGINNING Beginners
BRIGHT and EARLY BOOKS
for BEGINNING Beginners
BRIGHT and EARLY BOOKS
for BEGINNING Beginners
BRIGHT and EARLY BOOKS
for BEGINNING Beginners
BRIGHT and EARLY BOOKS
for BEGINNING Beginners
BRIGHT and EARLY BOOKS
for BEGINNING Beginners
BRIGHT and EARLY BOOKS
for BEGINNING Beginners
BRIGHT and EARLY BOOKS
for BEGINNING Beginners
BRIGHT and EARLY BOOKS
for BEGINNING Beginners